Skypunk Princess
Episode 2

This is a work of fiction. Similarities to real people, places, or events are entirely coincidental.

SKYPUNK PRINCESS

First edition. February 22, 2024.

ISBN: 979-8224731992

Written by David Colello.

By David Colello

1

For my north star, Meghan

Works By

David Colello

<u>Mission Cerex Series</u>
Trillion Dollar Sky
Diamond Disaster
Occator Unleashed
Rebel Uprising
Blue Moon
<u>Skypunk Princess Series</u>
Episode 1 (Mer Rescue)
Episode 2 (Paris Underground)
Episode 3 (The Leeches)
For a complete list, go to www.davidcolello.com[1].

---

1. http://www.davidcolello.com

Sometimes it takes a Princess with a plasma sword to pick up the pieces of a failed world. In the aftermath of climate disaster and the fall of human civilization, a brave few have formed new societies in harmony with nature. Now the AI cities are moving to eradicate these rebels. Eliana Skybound is an elite Sky Ranger, who charges into a swarm of drones with no fear. Her nanofabric wingsuit makes her a powerful force, but even she has her weaknesses.

Leva Kailani is a Mer Princess who has yet to fully choose her biohacked form, which makes her a fierce crystalline scaled distraction of the best kind.

After tragedy strikes, their love has a chance to remake the course of history, but only if they have the strength to endure.

Chapter 1

After getting assigned to rally as many Liminal communities as possible against the coming threat from Cyber, Eliana and Leva had exactly two days off. Then they were en route to Europe in the cramped interior of their Anemoi, an advanced craft resembling a sea urchin with its endless sensors, thrusters, and cannons.

After they reached the Continent, they met a contingent of Mer raiders, who smuggled them along the Seine and then through an endless series of moss clogged tunnels. Finally making it into ankle deep water in the sewers below New Paris, they left their escorts and continued on foot alone.

The pair stepped up onto the cobblestone bricks of an abandoned storm drain. There was a low domed ceiling that even Leva, who barely stood even with Eliana's shoulders, had to crouch under to move comfortably. But it was dry, and anything dry was good after their recent path.

Leva stalked forward, her shimmering green scales reflecting the torchlight wherever they peeked out from the nanoarmor.

"Time to suit up, Princess," Leva teased.

Elle had still been clinging to the hope that she was kidding about the dresses, but Lev always got her way. Out of their packs came a cloud of sheer blue cloth, matching floral Sky Ambassador togas, which they both promptly slipped over their armor. On this point Elle was quite insistent; they went nowhere without their nanosuits.

Unfortunately the armor also made tying the sash awkward, and Lev was still struggling once Elle finished with hers. She came up behind her partner, sliding hands passed Lev's hips with a practiced ease. As she grabbed the sash ends, unnatural silence descended around Elle.

"Lev, get down!"

A long metal spike trailed along Elle's face, brushing some stray hairs back out of the way. Lev had been pushed to the ground, but froze there when she saw someone holding Elle in a death grip.

"Nobody has to get hurt here," Eliana said calmly, as if a woman with razor lined armor plating wasn't holding what appeared to be a scorpion tail up under her chin.

Lev held her hands up in peace, but both held sleek black needle guns in their palms. "Now friend, my partner is right. We are on a diplomatic mission." She paused for effect. "So don't make me shoot you."

The scorpion woman flexed her deadly armor, which resembled Elle's nanoskin but with a more dramatic flair. She stood on four heavily protected legs, each splayed in a wide anchoring stance. The outer edges of her suit were all long knives, and her torso was covered with elaborate tech which was ingrained right into her leathery red skin.

The most obvious addition was a segmented tail which seemed to have a life of its own; it flicked around hypnotically, most of it looking black as wet tar, except for a series of purple streaks which pulsed with life and energy. Right now it came up under Elle's legs from behind, hovering an inch from her neck with a viciously sharp stinger.

"Didn't tell me there'd be two of you. Definitely didn't tell me about any Mer." As she stared at Leva she shifted to Elle's other shoulder, readjusting her grip on Elle's torso while her deadly tail kept its position.

"Click?" Leva asked incredulously.

Doubt crept across the scorpion woman's face in a brief flash, then resignation and a slight nod. "Who in hells did they send me?" Her hair, which had been the same fire red as her skin, transformed within seconds, doubling in length and cooling into a royal blue that was soon matched by her skin. "A Feather and a Fish?"

Eliana winked at Lev, then triggered her suit repulsion, which sent ten thousand volts through her exoskin and made an audible *pop* as it flung Click backwards into a nearby tunnel wall. The scorpion hybrid somehow managed to catch herself with two legs and used the momentum to propel back within striking distance, but then stopped short.

Slowly, two of Click's legs folded themselves flush against her back to form a bulging ridge ready to snap out on command. As they lifted up, Eliana noted what looked like turrets coming out of the soles of her boots. She stood with an easy swagger, her leathery armor transforming before their eyes into pale muscled skin, except the long rows of razor blades remained, likely anchored into her bones. In short, she was a nightmare with a crooked smile.

"Well then, that's better. Afraid Sky had sent me a couple of snowflakes."

Eliana positioned herself between Click and Leva, her dress burnt and smoldering in spots. "Where are your people?"

"My people? What do you want with us?"

"We bring a warning, for all the Liminal tribes. Cyber has broken the Peace, and we're all in danger."

The smile ran away from Click's face at the mention of Cyber. "The Peace? What Peace? Do you want to see what peace looks like here?"

While the scorpion woman backpedaled to a less threatening distance, Lev and Elle exchanged unsure glances, but she fit the rough description the Sky Council had given them, so they agreed to follow along. Click led the way, with Leva staying in back in case things went sideways.

The low ceiling of an abandoned drainage tunnel opened up into a wider room almost immediately, with the chalky limestone floor silencing the sound of their steps. But it was the walls that made Eliana grip her weapon tighter. From floor to ceiling, human skulls and bones were carefully stacked, making a grisly scene which stretched off into the distance.

Leva gasped when she saw the terrible sight, but Click barely seemed to notice. When the two newcomers fell behind, their guide let out a knowing laugh.

"Gods help me, they're long dead. If some catacombs are too scary for you, then maybe you should go fly home now."

Elle walked over and ran her fingers down over an embedded skull. "I've heard stories about humans from before the Singularity, but I just never imagined there could have been so many."

"So many...there must be thousands," Leva muttered, lost in a similar reverie.

"Millions," Click shrugged. "They're probably the only thing keeping Cyber from chasing us underground." She waved a hand around the hallway. "They seem to have a weird obsession with them. Which is ironic, because they don't seem to give a shit about us living humans."

They all fell silent for a minute as their little group made its way along the grim corridors. There were so many twists and turns that Elle had no clue how anyone could keep them straight. Whoever still used these passageways had left small electric lanterns every hundred feet or so, giving off just enough light to follow the path, but leaving large pools of shadow in between that were quickly filled by monsters of their imagination.

Thankfully, Click came to a halt, but nothing looked different about the tunnel. The skeletal architecture stretched on into the murky distance, but their guide was examining a particular group of skulls with a practiced hand, brushing over a femur that hadn't seen sunlight in hundreds of years. Then a smile turned up the corner of her thin lips as she pulled on a hidden lever, setting off a series of grinding stone movements. A circular hatch opened up in the roof of the tunnel, leaking an eerie blue light down around them.

"Follow me, no unnecessary sounds," Click ordered before nodding towards the wall of bones. Her extra two legs unfolded, their razor armor glinting in the unnatural glow from above, as she clambered up with ease.

Eliana looked at Leva and shrugged. "Stay behind me. Be ready to backtrack."

The metallic tail came back down through the hole, flicking upwards in invitation. Rather than step on the bones, Elle crouched down low before springing up past the tail and out of the tunnel.

Up above was a wasteland of ruined buildings. Instead of sunlight, there was only a sea of neon blue coming off the nearby shop signs, and four or five hundred feet up, a uniform gray ceiling stretched to every horizon. It was as if someone had built a second city on stilts over the old one. None of the buildings looked in use for a hundred years, yet each one was lit up like they were having a grand opening. A baker's holographic display still beckoned to hungry customers with a cartoonish figure in striped shirt and beret, but dust lay caked over the doorway. Despite the gaudy light shows, there appeared to be no one left alive, like an abandoned museum.

Elle glanced back down the opening to where Lev was climbing, and with one hand signed "all clear, but careful." Leva's dress was filthy already, but she still took special care to avoid tearing the fabric when it got snagged on a rib jutting out from the wall.

Click didn't wait to see if they followed, and ran in a gallop with all four legs pushing her on towards an imposing structure about fifty yards away. As Leva finally emerged up onto the street, her eyes nearly popped out of her skull in amazement.

Eliana took her lover's hand and tugged it insistently. Together they made slow progress towards the steel archway where Click had disappeared seconds earlier. Leva finally snapped back into focus, fighting the urge to drink in every detail of this animated ghost town.

Past the archway, they entered an enormous open air building, likely a transportation hub by the looks of the layout. Their guide was waiting impatiently inside an elevator near the back walls, so the pair of Princesses beelined over and joined her. The doors slid shut silently and efficiently as if they had just been installed that day.

Something was different, but it took Elle a moment to realize what it was. No dust. Click, for her part, did nothing to explain this, or at least she wasn't surprised by the change.

"Where the hell is she taking us?" Lev whispered before they stepped through the doors.

Elle flicked her hands behind her in rushed sign language, "not sure, stay ready."

Without windows, there was no way to tell how far up they traveled, but by the feel of the extra G force, it had to be high.

Leva nearly lifted up off the floor as they came to a stop, her dirt streaked dress billowing up into her face before she smoothed it back down, then quickly finished the job by pulling tight the sash belt.

Seconds passed but the doors remained closed. Click rolled her eyes and used her lethal tail to tap on a nearly invisible security camera positioned above and behind them.

"Let us in, Charon."

Silence. Then, as Leva was about to open her mouth came a disembodied voice around them, "no outsiders."

"I bring who I want, and you don't get to say shit about it, doorman." The last word dripped like poison from Click's thin lips, daring him to respond.

The doors slid open after another brief pause, and the scene was a beautiful chaos. Sunlight flooded a gargantuan platform suspended between three close set skyscrapers by suspension cables large enough to walk on. The platform was easily a few hundred feet above the dull gray metal ceiling they saw from ground level.

Whereas everything in the city beneath the gray layer had been gritty and abandoned, above it was a fantastical garden, with green straight on to the horizon in every direction. Flowering vines and towering trees filled the rooftops of any buildings taller than the false floor, with waterfalls showering down from above.

But despite the overwhelming splendor, the Princesses both took a step back after scanning what was happening on the platform ahead of them. A brawny man in full military fatigues holding a plasma rifle was being held aloft with an animal horn through his chest.

The horn belonged to a nightmarish creature nearly ten feet tall. When it reared up in victory and stood on two of its massive legs, a human face sneered from where its neck should have been. Cheers rose up from scattered pockets of people, some from dozens of fighters waiting on the outskirts of the platform, with still more coming out of windows and balconies in the surrounding buildings.

The rhino berserker waited at the center of the platform, letting loose a roar which vibrated the suspension cables all the way out to where Click now stood.

Eliana ignored the bellowing, but skipped out after Click onto the cable to get a better view of the city below. Still no movement from anything down near the gray dome. Leva followed after them, lining up each step with care. She was concentrating on the cable and didn't notice the hush fall over the crowd.

From behind the building to their right floated a strange shimmering bubble, massive but delicate looking. Sunlight refracted through what appeared to be hundreds of subdivisions. The rhino was bathed in a flood of rainbows, cutting his celebration short and enraging him further. As the bubble closed to within a hundred feet of the sneering giant, he grabbed a rifle off the bloodied commando at his feet and began firing a steady stream of plasma pulses.

While Click and Eliana trotted down the cable to get a closer view of the new action, Leva chose to drop down and straddle the steel rather than tempt fate.

Instead of shredding the incoming bubble into mist, the pulses sailed right through as if they were no more troublesome than a gust of wind.

Closer and closer it floated, neither speeding up or slowing down, just tracking inexorably towards the now concerned would-be-champion. When it reached the platform, the rhino charged at it in a blind fury but did no more damage than the plasma rifle.

Instead of recoiling from this violence, the bubble slid itself around the burly fighter while morphing into a series of concentric spheres. Even the rhino's increasingly frantic screams became muted, then vanished entirely behind layer after layer of mostly translucent glimmer. Once encased, no amount of flailing or striking out seemed to do any damage.

Then the gas began to form. What had been clear air seconds earlier in the space surrounding the rhino began filling itself with a strange green fog. The eyes bulged in impotent fury as the champion kicked and slashed at the endless layers which were beginning to suffocate him. The sickly cloud grew denser, causing armor to erode and skin to slough off until the great beastly fighter dropped to the platform, convulsing in helpless death throes.

The whole process had taken less than a minute, and it took even less time for the bubble creature to absorb the acid fog and slide off the mountain of flesh and bone. Layer after layer popped into innocent sprays of shimmering mist.

Then from the inner recesses of the central membranes there suddenly emerged a naked sprite of a woman, no more than a foot tall, who was emitting a gentle green glow. The tiny warrior floated on a single bubble to the center of the platform and let out a shrill cry, challenging anyone else who dared.

After a long pause with everyone staring at the pixie in respectful silence, a crystal spire began growing up from an opening in the dome far below. Eliana glanced back to make sure Leva was still safe, then slid down the cable for a closer look. The glimmering monolith came all the way up and extended up through the center of the arena. When it reached roughly twenty feet above the platform, it gradually stopped.

Branches grew out from all sides and heights, spiraling in fractal beauty, and from the tips of each there appeared glassy fruits.

The pixie took this all in stride and touched her diminutive hand up against the base of the trunk, causing all the fruits to fall to the ground. As she picked up her prizes, the tree was already receding back down into the platform, and the onlooking crowd dispersed.

Chapter 2

"What the hell was that?" Elle raised an eyebrow in Click's direction. The scorpion woman didn't turn right away, her gaze still fixed on the pixie as if trying to solve a puzzle.

"The peace," she said finally, "Cyber sets these matches up and lets us fight for scraps while they watch."

"Why do they even care?"

Click rolled her eyes. "Cyber's not just bolts and wires anymore, you know? They got kinks like humans now, I guess. Watching the meat puppets kill each other is fun for them, or at least some of them. I think they mainly do it as a relief valve."

"Let us kill each other so we don't turn on them?"

"More or less."

"You fight, too?" Eliana sized up her guide with fresh eyes, wondering what she was capable of.

"Only when I can win." She turned her gaze to the bubble floating off out of sight. "And that tiny thing has never been beaten, so I watch."

"Smart play." Eliana's gaze wandered off towards the pixie as well.

Click tapped her now cherry red hair and smirked, "I may not look like it, but I have the latest supercomp software up here."

"You turning Cyber?" Elle asked, stone faced.

"Nah, still me up there. Just a whole shit ton more of me." Then after a pause, "what the hell's your girlfriend up to, anyway?"

That's when Elle looked back up the cable to where she left Leva before the fight. They had a hard link comm implanted, so she wasn't worried since she hadn't heard any commotion, but then again, when Leva was quiet she was usually up to something.

At first she saw nothing, but then a pair of bare feet came into focus, one on each side of the cable about 50 feet away. Lev had chosen not to get her Mer tail, and she insisted on feeling everything she could with her hard fought for legs. Right now those legs were upside down and clamped around the enormous cable, with each foot hooking over the top of a side for extra strength.

Eliana sighed and stepped off into the air hundreds of feet above the hard grey shell below. The cape from her matte black nanosuit flared out into a cone around her legs, halting her descent as powerful ionic jets kicked into action.

Leva gave a lopsided smile as Elle hovered next to her. Her cropped platinum hair whipped in the steady wind gusts as she was squinting down below. Her dress flopped down around her, leaving her green scaled legs glinting brilliantly.

Eliana's gaze lingered on her fearless companion, always impressed by her energy, then turned downward to figure out what they were looking at. While Leva's eyes were not enhanced like her own, Eliana couldn't pick out anything noteworthy at first. Her telescopic irises engaged on command and gave her hundreds of times more detail and magnification.

Even then it was easy to miss the tiny figure moving steadily across the top of the grey dome. Elle reached out a forearm and a tiny cloud of nanodrones puffed out, immediately racing downward at her command.

"What is that?" she asked Leva, but by now Click had strided over, and answered first.

"More of a who than a what, but just barely."

Both Princesses snapped out of their focused staring and turned up to face Click, waiting for more explanation.

"The Banished, they were AI once upon a time. Well, still are I suppose, but they fucked up."

"And now?"

"Now they're trapped in a metal suit, cut off from the rest of the Singularity, and forced to walk alone on top of the AI city."

"That's so sad," Leva cut in, her face flush from hanging upside down for so long.

Neither Click nor Elle seemed similarly moved. The nanodrones had reached their target, giving a close up view of a bizarre creature moving in slow motion, which Elle shared with the group by swiping across her forearm towards the air between them.

The Banished appeared in the holo, a rigid blocky metal contraption that gave out anguished screeches of grinding metal as it walked along. Its legs were single hinged chunks of steel, and slender rods with crude pincers hung down straight for its arms. The only thing hinting that it was more than a forgotten trash bot was a glowing orb of light resting on top.

Without another word Leva released her grip on the cable and plummeted into the emptiness beneath them.

"What the hell?!" Click moved an arm out in vain to catch her, but she was already fifty feet down and accelerating.

Eliana sighed through a smile, "she has a bad habit of doing this. We'll meet you back down at the catacombs." Her ion jet skirting ceased, dropping her like a hawk in chase of its prey. As her wavy black hair whipped into a riot around her, she heard Click call something out to her, but it was lost in the wind.

Turning her gaze downward, she caught sight of Leva's shimmering bodysuit just before a nanosteel parachute emerged out from flat tubes along her spine. She swirled in graceful loops, thoroughly enjoying her flight until stumbling on the landing and face planting on the gray metal.

"Ooooh, still getting used to your new toy?" Elle had insisted on a nanosuit for Leva after almost losing her during the Drone City attacks. It was only a week since they had defeated the AI megaship that was traveling across the Atlantic, but it seemed like a different lifetime. Lazy sundrenched days before the Cyber attack, with Leva tying Mer jewelry into her hair, had now changed to diplomatic missions into war zones.

Leva sprung back to her feet like a gymnast, more embarrassed than injured. "Yeah, noticed you didn't get them to spring for any fancy jet suit for me."

"Not enough time, sorry love. You know you can actually let me know before flinging yourself off high buildings though, right?"

"Where's the fun in that?"

Elle shook her head in resignation, walking over to the Banished, who had continued its glacial march without so much as turning its head. "It does seem sad, if AI can be sad, that is. Wonder what crime a bot has to do to get itself unplugged?"

Leva glided closer for a better look. Considering she only had a couple years of total time walking on land, she always astonished Elle by moving more gracefully than most unmodded humans. "I can't imagine any crimes a Cyber could even be capable of. Aren't they practically one collective mind?"

"Maybe that was its crime, doing something on its own?"

Leva had a giggle escape her grinning mouth, "rogue Cyber, roaming the desolate grayscape, exploring mysteries..."

Eliana smirked, "at this rate it's gonna be a few millennia before it explores this square mile."

Leva took off a nanomesh glove as she neared the Banished.

"Leva, what are you doing?"

"Not sure," she responded, her tone turning more serious. She slowly reached her green scaled hand out towards the nearest rod arm, touching it lightly, but nothing happened.

"Alright, let's go Lev."

As the Mer turned to face her, Eliana watched the Banished rise up nearly four feet taller and aim its stubby metal arm towards them. An anguished screeching siren came out of where its mouth should be, followed by an electric flash erupting down its arm. As the arc of plasma streaked past Lev's ear, Eliana's world flashed red, and the next thing she knew the siren stopped as suddenly as it began.

She smelled a whiff of ozone and glanced down at the daggerlion pointing out from her hip, then followed its path towards the heap of melted scrap that used to be the Banished. Several fist sized holes riddled its head and body, each one having carved a neat path through the ancient creature.

Lev felt the singed blonde hair brush her cheek, then gasped as she saw the wreckage behind her.

"Holy shit, what was that?" she stammered.

"Time to go," was all Eliana said, and there were numerous far off sirens helping to make her case.

The women grabbed each other's arms and set off towards the nearest skyscraper, hoping for another elevator down. When they reached their destination, they were greeted by a solid gray wall as far up as they could see.

Another spray of plasma bursts bit into metal nearby, and Eliana shoved Lev down to the floor behind her.

"Stay put, stay low!" she ordered Lev, then sprinted towards an incoming stream of drones.

Dozens were streaking out of a hatch less than a hundred yards away, but Eliana worked to close the distance. Her upgraded suit was being put to use sooner than she had hoped. Her nanosilk cape billowed out in front of her, forming a translucent shield which deflected the incoming pulses with ease. She ran with her daggerlion blade trailing down by her side, ready to pounce at the drone vanguard.

Her arms were a blur as seven heaps of metal crashed to the desolate gray landscape. After the initial wave, she slid down on her knees, whipping both arms out to her sides along with swarms of needle sized missiles, each bending its path toward the nearest target. Ten more drones skittered down harmlessly and Eliana spun on her knees to follow the remainder who were now on their way past her to the easier target huddled low to the ground.

Her cape retracted itself as Elle brought up her daggerlion with deadly aim. The end of her weapon sparked rapidly as EM pulses each found their mark, and within seconds the entire attacking drone patrol lay scattered in useless heaps between the two women.

Lev was up and running, but not at Elle, and not at the surrounding buildings either. She turned and waved at Elle to follow her lead, which she did immediately. By the time Elle caught up, Lev was pushing a hatch panel open, a slight rim of rust hinting at its purpose. Water trickled from the surrounding area on a barely noticeable decline, pooling a bit around the edges.

When the hatch opened fully, Lev gasped slightly and fell back on her butt. Eliana peeked through and saw a dim expanse reaching far beneath them.

"Not a great time to develop a fear of heights, my little minnow." Eliana dropped her guard enough to wink, then edged past Lev to stick her head down into the hatch for a better view. After a moment to scan for any immediate dangers, she lifted her head back out.

"Bottoms up, backup won't be far behind." And with that, Elle dove through the hatch, only hesitating to wiggle her hips through the tight squeeze. As her cape and feet swooshed out of sight, Leva did an equipment check to make sure her chute was properly retracted back in its tubes, then peeked down after her.

As soon as her shoulders edged past the opening, Eliana's hand popped up and grabbed the nanomesh of her chest plate, pulling her through the rest of the way. They tumbled for a few meters, exposed circuitry and rusting gray metal spinning around them until Leva settled into a straddle of Elle's left hip, her legs locking in place just before the cape shot out beneath them. Stabilizing into the familiar cone jets around their legs, her cape adjusted to accommodate the extra passenger.

The gray dome was only about twenty feet thick, with the underside offering no new features to examine. It merely stretched out to the horizon in a dull expanse which angled itself down well past the city limits of Old Paris. The neon blues and reds took over again as they descended and looked for a place to land. On the far side of the city the Eiffel Tower lay broken in half sideways by the dull gray ceiling. Finally spotting the building where they first entered with Click, Eliana set them down gently.

Before they could look around for a hiding spot, a flattened metal tail whipped through both their legs, sending them tumbling asses over elbows into an undignified heap on the concrete.

"Get up Princesses!" Click was fuming, all four armored legs pacing around them. "Time to get underground before the swarm comes."

Elle was back on her feet first, stepping between Leva and the enraged woman. "What swarm?"

"Don't get cute with me. I heard the alarm." Click started stalking off towards a nearby building that was crumbling from decades of neglect. Over her shoulder she continued her rant. "What the hell did you do? Mess with the Banished?"

Elle and Leva were reluctantly following her, taking care to stay out of reach of her tail, which was twitching violently behind her as she went. "Calm down, alright?" Eliana attempted to reason with her, "There was a little incident, but we handled it."

Click reached the ruined building and turned, glaring acid eyes at the pair. "You handled it, huh? Get in!" She gestured at what looked like a crevice between two fallen pillars.

Elle stopped and put an arm across Leva's chest to hold her back. "We're not going anywhere until you explain."

"No time for that."

"And why not?"

"That's why," Click answered, pointing up at the ever present gray dome. As they all watched, a low buzzing sound began to fill the air in all directions.

At first nothing else appeared to happen, then suddenly Elle jumped a few inches back. "What is that?" she asked, Leva still confusedly looking around.

Eliana held a forearm up in front of Leva, and a small screen popped up from it. Through the enhanced HUD, Lev saw the dome coming to life, seeming to rain down tiny fireflies of electronic signatures.

"That's the Swarm," was all Click explained before shimmying her awkward frame between the pillars.

The Princesses quickly followed, dropping through seconds before an ear piercing screech filled the city. Click hit some hidden panel and the pillars collapsed against each other, sealing them underground.

Chapter 3

Click took the lead, scurrying down a decline path strewn with broken cobblestone. What began as a cramped tunnel where they all had to duck down, gradually opened up wider and taller until the three of them were quickly jogging in the near pitch blackness. Click and Eliana both had enhanced vision, but Leva was struggling along, clinging to Elle's arm, nearly falling multiple times until finally deciding to stop.

"Are you alright?" Elle asked in a hushed tone. However, the response was anything but quiet.

"Where the fuck are you taking us?" Leva snapped at their scorpion guide.

"Please, you must be quiet, just another minute, then I'll answer your questions," she answered, a note of pleading creeping into her voice.

Then she turned to Eliana. "We're coming to an EMP shield. If you need to shut down any systems, now is the time." The Sky warrior hesitated, but then tapped out a series of commands on an arm console, which in turn caused multiple streaks of light along her nanosuit to dim before blinking off. She did the same for Leva's suit, then turned back to follow Click.

The cobblestone was nearly thirty feet wide here, with twin ruts running along the center. Suddenly Elle realized they must be walking an ancient street of Old Paris. Side tunnels branched off at regular intersections, but up ahead was a crude sewer manhole, and Click was heading straight for it.

With one powerful arm, Click lifted the heavy iron cover off and set it gently on the street, barely making a sound. The three of them climbed down on a rusty ladder, Leva going last. As they descended, the hairs on the back of Leva's neck stood up, and she began to feel a bit dizzy.

Eliana noticed her wavering above her. "Try to keep moving, it's already lessening where I am." But Leva barely registered her lover's voice. She tilted back and was jarred into focus by her shoulders impacting the wet stone walls.

Managing to resume her grip on the ladder rungs while bracing against the stone for support, she forced herself down a few more steps. Sure enough, the dizziness passed. Her feet touched down on a wide rock slab a few seconds later, and Elle had her sit down to recover.

When she turned to Click, her voice had a controlled edge to it which caused their guide to stop at last. "Start...explaining," was all she had to say.

Click folded her second pair of legs up into the cavity along her back, slowly so as not to give Eliana any reason to doubt her intentions, and sat down several feet from them.

"Welcome to Gèoville," she offered with a forced smile, "well, the entrance anyways." Both Princesses glanced at each other doubtfully. Click simply grinned and motioned with both hands to be calm and then muttered, "lumière." Bright blue LEDs flashed into action all around them, streaking along the crude tunnel which led away from the ladder and looked to be cut out of solid stone.

Finally able to see again for the first time since they hid underground, Leva stood and threw a hand to the gun on her thigh, staring daggers at Click. "Explain more, bitch."

Laughter rang out in the tunnel, as Click relaxed her own stance, seemingly no longer afraid of making noise. "Feisty one, isn't she?" Eliana almost nodded in sympathy before catching herself, checking to see if Leva noticed the near slip up.

Click continued, "let's see, a recap. You two crawled out of the river into our sewers. I was giving you a tour, which I only agreed to do, mind you, because I haven't seen a new human face in forever. Then you decided to jump off a skyscraper, break the Truce which has held for over a decade, and triggered a Swarm which is going to make providing for our people nearly impossible for a while."

After neither Princess said anything for a few seconds, Click leaned back on her hands, "And now here we are."

Eliana resumed her stoic posture first. "We had no idea touching that scrap of metal would trigger such a massive response." After a brief pause she continued, "but for our part in your people's suffering, we are both very sorry." Eliana turned to face Leva, and waited, until Click too turned to stare. Leva finally relented, relaxing her face before nodding her agreement.

Click blew air through her lips. "Apologies from royalty, I feel honored." Before they could bristle too much at the comment she said, "Maybe it was inevitable, the Swarm. If what you say is true, Cyber may have gotten tired of tolerating humans."

"How many of you are down here?" Lev asked.

Click motioned for them to follow her again. "Come see for yourself."

She turned a corner up ahead of them and leapt down a large flight of stairs three at a time. At the bottom was a massive man, nearly seven feet tall with shoulders that completely filled the doorway he stood in. His body was covered in black metal armor plating that reflected the sparse lighting, but his hands were what drew Eliana's attention. Or rather, what had replaced his hands.

"Ladies, meet Melter." Click jumped up and gave him a quick peck on his cheek, making him blush slightly. "He's a gentleman, but...no shaking hands."

The Princesses both nodded in deference to the mountain of a bodyguard, while Eliana kept staring at the glowing circles at the end of his arms.

"Dual fusion cores," Melter's voice came out softer than Elle ever would have imagined.

"May I?" she smiled at him, obviously still curious.

He lifted them out, part cutting edge tech and part medieval cudgel, but motioned for them not to touch.

"Amazing work. You made these?" Elle asked.

Melter laughed, "Me, no. Won them in the sky fights." After motioning them to step back, he made a lightning quick sideways jab, faster than anyone his size should be able to move, driving one glowing fist into the wall. It sank more than a foot into the formerly solid stone, pushing molten slag out dripping to the floor.

Leva strutted right up to the giant and patted him hard on the shoulder. "Glad you're on our side," she deadpanned, then walked past him and through the doorway.

Whatever she was expecting to see, this wasn't it. Leva's eyes glazed over at the immensity of the cavern in front of her. They were at the ceiling, with naturally formed columns stretching down for hundreds of feet, while platforms dotted the landscape at all levels. Rope ladders connected some areas, crude metal bridges spanned gaps, and throughout them all cascaded a series of minor waterfalls which sent mist billowing up. A single thread of golden sunlight shared its warmth and glow to the entire cavern, using mirrors to direct the pathway in crisscrossing patterns, ending far below and out of sight from where they stood.

There were people moving among the platforms, not in huge amounts, but noticeable even from their height. Click watched their reaction carefully before explaining, "a few hundred of us are left down here."

"So many?" Leva gasped.

"So few." Click gazed off into the distance. "Every year we lose more to patrols, rockslides...and starvation."

"Don't you have hydroponic farms?" Eliana prodded gently.

"Of course, but the system is old. Parts break down, and aren't so easily replaced. That's why some of us fight."

They began moving along the pathways downward in silence for a minute, passing a few others who stared wide eyed at the strangers. The Géos were pale, and moved with a monotony born from years of hiding.

"Why are you here at all?" Leva asked. "I'm sorry, I don't mean to offend you, but...this doesn't seem like a sustainable...anything.

Click laughed, but her face didn't. "Not everyone had the chance to just swim away like you, little guppy."

Leva bristled, but Elle held her back with a hand and a look. "Lev, the Singularity trapped millions in cities suddenly controlled by AI. Cyber didn't exactly warn humanity before they took control." Then to Click she asked, "There's no way to get these people out?"

"Not easily. We could try burrowing out beyond the city limits, and hope they don't monitor much outside the Dome. But that would take years, decades even, and then what? Where would we even go?" She shook her head in defeat. "No, this is our fate."

As she finished speaking, the group came out from behind a large stone pillar, and another surprise greeted the newcomers. They could finally see the bottom of the cavern, a sprawling shallow pool of water collecting from the drips and gurgling waterfalls, and at its center there was a raised circle of land. Polished black rocks were carefully arranged in intricate symbols around a central dias, which was the final destination of the beam of sunlight ricocheted around the massive cavern. And there, glistening with mist were hundreds of sweet purple irises clinging to life, crowding close to stay in the column of brightness.

Leva stared in silent reverie at the beautiful little sanctuary, stopping to lean far out over the rope bridge they were crossing. Eliana was taken aback as well, but pressed on following their guide, tugging the Mer along behind her.

Ahead of them they saw one of the cavern walls had been cut, forming dozens of shallow open caves where people huddled. In the shallow water beneath, several children chased a hollow plastic sphere as it skipped along leaving splashes of dirty water in its wake.

Leva took a momentary glance back at Elle before bounding off to play with the children, her powerful body propelling her so fast it looked like she sped across the water itself. A smile twitched at the edges of Eliana's mouth as she watched, then she turned to Click.

"If we can help, would you-" but Click cut her off.

"Don't. Please don't do that. You barely know us, and in the time you have, you've already almost got me killed." She looked away, down towards the lit field of flowers. "You've done enough."

"The Sky Council sent us to contact any settlements we can find, and to help them if we can. We're going to need every human left alive in order to defeat Cyber."

Silence stretched out between them as the pair watched Leva dive headfirst into a crowd of laughing kids.

"But more importantly," she smirked, "we're stubborn as hell."

Click muttered something too soft for even Eliana's ears to pick up, then let out a long hiss. "I haven't seen kids laugh like that in years. Your woman is special, and for that I'll hear you out." She turned and lightly shoved Elle's shoulders back. "No promises, understood?"

"Of course."

"This better be good."

The next hour involved plenty of quiet discussions with Click, the Princesses shooting down objections and refusing to let their plan die. Eventually the scorpion woman relented, and agreed to talk with their Elders.

"This will take some time. Many of the Elders were born before the Singularity. We've got them some nano from time to time, but," she threw her hands up and smiled, "they're just old."

Before she left, she brought them to an offshoot cave, much deeper down, where the rock began to feel warmer and sounds of the waterfalls faded to a distant hum. In its place came a clashing of metal and desperate yells. Click motioned for calm, then led them through a small circular hole into another massive room. A couple dozen people were watching as two arena fighters clashed near the far wall.

"So you don't get bored," she said, and turned to walk back the way they had come in.

As she stepped out through the circular door, she called out, "Let's show these Princesses some hospitality! But be nice, the Elders might need to speak to them." One last wink, and Click was gone.

Absolutely everyone stopped and turned towards them, the two fighters even breaking off mid-punch. They formed a crowd to gain confidence, but still no one seemed to want to volunteer as leader. Eliana stepped forward to take control of the situation.

"Hello, we didn't mean to interrupt. Please continue."

But no one backed away. Then a deeply scarred man with four arms and hair down to his shoulders lifted his voice above the murmurs. "Here you must fight to earn the right to speak."

As if anticipating this, Eliana's lips pulled back into a feral grin, a warrior's impulse building inside her wanting to pummel someone up close where she could hear the impact of her fists. But the man shook his head.

"Not you. The little one."

Leva stepped out from behind Elle and cocked her head to the side. "Did he just call me little?"

Eliana shrugged. "I believe he did." Then she looked back and forth between Leva and the bare chested challenger.

"Shirtless? C'mon, that's a bit cliche," Leva quipped. "You're gonna get sweat all over.

Now it was the man's turn to shrug, lifting all four arms in the air. "It's hard finding clothes that fit."

"Preach. Well, here I am talking my ass off. Let's get on with this."

They both walked into a clearing made by the crowd who had begun making bets. Leva had her nanosuit on, so Elle seemed cautiously optimistic, as long as Leva remembered the basic techniques they practiced and kept her guard up.

"So do we count down or something, or do we-" the rest of Leva's question was cut off as she was lifted up by a surging attack, then thrown down again by a second pair of arms. She bounced off the hard stone floor, her hair splayed out and clinging to the wet surface as she gasped to catch her breath.

The triumphant four armed man turned his back and began to strut in front of his friends. Just as Eliana was about to intervene, Leva pushed herself back up into a crouch.

Before the man even had a chance to turn around, alerted by the startled eyes of the crowd, Leva had closed the distance between them and leapt feet first. Her boots landed hard on the man's calves, buckling his legs. Immediately she planted her own shoulder into the small of his back and grabbed hold of his long hair with both tiny fists. Her suit flared into action as its outer material hardened into ballistic grade carbon nanotubes.

"Goro," the newly immobilized man said. None of his arms could reach back far enough, and hair was straining to stay in his scalp. "That's my name."

Leva stepped off his calves and kicked him away. "No, your name is Pits. God, I don't think I could have stayed that close for much longer."

Goro let out a deep bass laugh. "Yes, my apologies lit-...Princess."

Leva gave a quick curtsy and strutted back to Eliana, who gave a few mini claps in approval.

Elle turned to the rest of the group. "Now if everyone is done dicking around, we have a plan to save your sorry asses, so listen up."

Chapter 4

The Elders were not as easy to convince. Despite many fighters coming to vouch for their skills, most notably Click, they were not going to throw their people's lives away for a couple of outsiders.

Their plan sounded like lunacy anyways. Eliana and Leva promised to take down the entire city's defenses, by themselves, leaving a window of time when they could escape Géoville up into the city.

The most the Elders resigned themselves to doing was alert all of their people to pack their meager belongings. In their minds, between the already present Swarm and whatever foolishness the two Princesses had planned, Cyber might be goaded into attacking Géoville in force. If this happened they would all have to retreat into smaller offshoot caves and collapse the cavern with explosives.

In truth, they would have stopped the pair by force if they thought they could, but rumors of the Sky Rangers had even reached down to their community over the years. Perhaps they held out a bit of hope for their success, but if that was the case, their send off didn't reflect it. When it was time for Elle and Leva to head out, not a single person was allowed to accompany them.

Click led them back up to the sewer grate, having gone over their most likely routes up through the Dome. When she was finished, she put a hand on each of their shoulders.

"Don't worry," she gripped tighter to emphasize her words. "The Elders worry, and that is what has kept us alive for decades, but the fighters will have the people ready to move if you give us the chance."

"When," Eliana corrected her, eliciting a smile from their guide.

"When." Click made a slight bow, then scurried off on her four powerful legs back down towards Géoville.

Leva sighed, "Just you and I again, Feather."

Eliana leaned over and kissed her, pulling her waist in tight, and held her there even after their lips parted. "Ready to do something stupid, Fish?"

They took a new path up to the surface, silently following Click's instructions. Following a tunnel which led them under the Old City, they navigated back to the endless Catacombs. The bones gave an even more ominous feel than usual due to a low buzzing tone which had been getting louder as they neared the surface.

After groping around for the bone lever Click had painstakingly described how to find, Eliana pulled it and heard the deep grinding of stone on stone as a hatch slid open above them. As it did, an immense crash of sound assaulted them.

Elle jumped up and grabbed hold of the edge of the hatch, lifting herself until she could see outside, then cursed quietly before dropping back down. Offering Lev a foothold with her joined hands, she hoisted the Mer up to see for herself.

If not for the ever present darkness under the Dome, the sight wouldn't have been nearly as impressive. Leva looked out and saw a hurricane of stars, pinpricks of light swirling in a hectic yet ordered pattern. With the archaic neon signs of Paris adding their own vivid colors as a backdrop, the whole scene was a confusing galaxy of swirling light.

As the noise pushed down on Leva, jumbling her thoughts and making her want to climb back down underground, Eliana grabbed hold of her feet and pushed her up and out of the hatch. The Sky Ranger quickly jumped up beside her, clearing up and out in a single leap.

Fortunately, Click had steered them towards a safe exit point. They stood a few feet from what once was a VR parlor, its storefront displaying a hologram opening and closing her legs while wearing a bulky headset and nothing else. There was a long overhang with one way mirrors blocking the drones overhead from seeing them. The store's added steps to provide discretion to its customers made a perfect spot for the Princesses to exit the Catacombs and get their bearings.

"There's so many, too many," Leva muttered, half to Elle and half to herself.

But Eliana was already tapping out orders on her armband. Her nanosuit rapidly shifted, stretching up and over her hair and down across her face, only leaving openings to see, hear, and breathe. Then in a blink, she disappeared. Or nearly so. Adaptive optic displays made her virtually invisible, a slightly blurred background and the few bits of skin not covered were the only sign of her left.

"Holy shit!" Leva said, too loudly, then switched to a yelled whisper. "Holy shit, does mine do that?" Suddenly she squealed as an unseen hand traced it's fingers along the backs of her thighs.

Eliana's floating lips formed a wicked grin before answering. "It does. Not quite as well as mine, but it'll do."

"Do it, do mine!" She bounced excitedly before holding out her arms. Elle took one forearm and entered the appropriate commands, then watched as Leva's suit stretched itself around her. Rather than showing an exact copy of the view behind her, the lesser suit displayed a blurred outline, but only a close inspection would notice something was amiss.

Far above them, nearly too small to be seen, there was an opening. Eliana had spotted it during her lengthy examination of the latest maps Click had provided. While the people of Géoville could do little about defeating Cyber themselves, the fighters and scouts made it a point of honor to know every detail possible about them, not least of which was in support of their smuggling operations.

Unfortunately, in between the Princesses and their escape hatch flew thousands of drones, and even as invisible as the women were, the pair were bound to be detected by quite a few advanced sensors and other nanotech cloud layers.

Eliana quickly clipped a tether onto Leva and watched as the fabric fused into her nanosuit. Then she stepped forward, held the Mer close, and waited for the signal.

Click hadn't mentioned exactly what that signal would be, only that she promised to give them a fighting chance to escape. As they were learning with each passing hour, their scorpion guide was always full of surprises, and anything but subtle.

They weren't waiting long before an explosion echoed through the neon city streets. Before they could pinpoint exactly where it originated, another deafening boom came, along with a burst of wind from a shockwave rushing past them. This one was much closer, no more than a few blocks away, and was followed by the creaking of steel girders as a several story high building began to collapse.

Behind them another boom, then another, and Eliana jumped up before engaging her ion jets. The pair rocketed up into the perpetual night. As they cleared the level of most of the surrounding roofs, blossoming fireballs greeted their eyes in every direction. Leva clung on desperately to Elle, the tether not helping her relax much as they rocketed up into the open where thousands of drones were searching for them.

Only the drones were gone. At least at first, all the microdrones of the Swarm had reacted to the ring of explosions, leaving a vast and expanding clearing roughly centered around their location. Only a handful of stationary sentinels remained, and the women's suits seemed to be hiding them sufficiently.

Elle had them weaving upwards in a corkscrew, careful not to stray too close, when a tiny bot, no larger than a bee, impacted Leva's arm and shattered. But not before triggering a proximity alarm.

All as one, the thousands of drones which were rushing elsewhere stopped. After a moment of receiving new orders, they sped back towards the pair, this time having a much better idea where to find them. Eliana pushed her suit harder, beginning evasive maneuvers, and while the Swarm was closing in, they were still doing so at the location of their collision. The nanosuits' adaptive optics let them climb away from the rapidly shrinking clear skies, their disguises preventing utter disaster.

They reached their target less than a minute later, and shielded their eyes as the blinding glare of a morning sun pierced the small drainage hole. Pausing to ensure they were not spotted, the Princesses climbed through the narrow opening and stood in the warm glow of the sun.

From there the dangers seemed to disappear, the Swarm content to remain under the Dome. The pair jetted upwards once again, this time arcing around the few nearby skyscrapers to further mask their presence. A minute later they were piercing the low hanging cloud banks. Leva extended her arms out like wings as they flew, closing her eyes and dreaming on their way up to the Anemoi waiting for them right where they had left it.

"Sure this is a good idea?" Leva asked before stepping into the small cavity that was revealed once the ships' numerous ten foot spikes had parted.

Eliana waited until Leva had safely entered the cockpit and detached herself from the tether between them. "Whether it is or not I've been more than patient." The warrior smirked as she canceled her suits' camouflage. "No more hiding."

Elle blew a kiss to Leva before tilting into a graceful back dive, speeding quickly out of sight amidst the clouds.

"So dramatic." Leva rolled her eyes as the hatch closed and the countless spines resumed their formation.

Once Eliana cleared the cloud ceiling, she reached behind her where a sleek black sheath was attached to her suit. Out came her daggerlion, a wickedly sharp blade, which also contained some advanced nanotech. After holding it above her head, she triggered a button along the handle, causing a bloom of synthetic fibers to spring out in all directions. Using fluctuations in the electric field ever present in the atmosphere, the daggerlion captured the energy and emitted it through ionic bursts at her discretion.

Her descent slowed as she found her target, aiming herself down to fly between the few remaining skyscrapers. The huge triangular platform came into view as she passed the shining penthouse windows of the nearest tower. With all the commotion down below the dome, the fighting arena was left deserted for the most part.

She retracted her daggerlion just as her boots touched down gracefully on the scarred metal surface. A quick scan spotted a small patrol of a dozen or so reconnaissance drones flying in a lazy circle above her.

Her head bowed momentarily, drawing a slow and deep breath across her lips. When she raised her eyes up again, a fiery joy filled them. Her body sprung into action, lifting her daggerlion up even as its end was transforming into an EMP rifle. With practiced ease she pulled the trigger, knocking several of the drones out of the sky before they knew what hit them. The remaining handful hesitated, unsure whether to attack or flee the solitary figure. That moment of indecision was more than Elle needed.

The last drone skittered to rest on the edge of the arena, having barely managed to set off a general alarm. The Sky Ranger casually sheathed her weapon and sat down in a lotus position. Her cape flared into a wide inverted dome, soaking up the sunlight into its matte black surface. Her breathing was steady, eyes closed, drinking in her surroundings.

From far off came a high pitched hum as the massive chains holding each corner of the triangle began to vibrate. From the surrounding buildings were pouring thousands of Cyber bots, but unlike the earlier patrol, these were bristling with assorted weaponry. Down they came, jumping the last few yards off the chains and speeding inwards to where Eliana waited.

She stood up and watched the growing riot of machinery with little concern. A quick mental command sent the cape up and around her to form a wall just in time to deflect some lucky incoming shots. And there she stayed, hidden behind her bulletproof cape, as they clattered ever closer. Soon the entire arena was covered in a writhing mass of robotics, and still, Eliana hid. The leading bots were charging up their weapons, leaning forward in anticipation of an easy kill.

And then she was gone.

In her place was a narrow hole through the platform Elle had carved out while out of sight. The bots had way too much momentum built up by the time they saw their prey vanish, and so several dozen met an ignoble end smashed against each other, their parts falling down like metal rain through the hole.

Eliana smirked as she triggered her cape and jetted off towards the edge of the platform. When she reached one of the assignment chain supports, she allowed herself a glance backwards. Only a hundred or so Cyber were managing to climb down after her and cling to the underside, but even those few were making very slow progress in pursuit.

Elle hovered there watching them for a moment, then flicked her daggerlion back out. She ran her gloved fingers along the razor edge, savoring the moment before the carnage truly began. She was secretly glad that Leva rarely saw her this way, vicious in the way only true warriors can be.

The chain let out a terrifying groan as Elle's first strike severed halfway through a link. Her blade swept back up in an efficient arc, no wasted movement, cutting a clean line across the weathered steel.

"No mercy," she muttered as the corners of her mouth curled upwards. One final overhand strike sent the giant tether rebounding backwards with such force that it demolished an entire floor of the skyscraper which held it. The top of the building listed dangerously to the side, fire bellowing out from the gaping wound, but no one was looking in its direction to notice. That's because one corner of the triangle arena was in freefall along with thousands of Cyber shock troops. An avalanche of flailing bots slid off the newly vertical surface, peppering the dome beneath them in an endless series of small explosions.

The two chains managed to shoulder their burden, looking like a pendant necklace hanging between the two undamaged skyscrapers. When Eliana was done watching the destruction she had wrought, she flew over to the ten foot wide edge which now served as the only remaining place to stand on the infamous arena.

"Challenge!" She let out a controlled scream. "I demand a worthy challenge!" Now she paced along, letting her extended daggerlion scrape along the metal beams, letting out an agonizing screech of scratching metal and the occasional burst of sparks as she cut across an exposed bundle of wires.

Suddenly an overpowering voice shook Eliana, the platform, and the very air, shattering dozens of windows and causing the Sky Princess to take a knee for a moment.

"Your challenge...is accepted."

Elle sighed in relief. 'Step one complete,' she thought, 'now for the hard part.'

Chapter 5

Silence descended after the pronouncement, and no new swarm came to attack her. What did emerge was a ten foot tall behemoth, a feminine looking Cyber warrior, who was striding confidently down the chain to Elle's right. Its entire body was encased in a smooth nanosteel shell that gleamed white in the sun. As it approached, Eliana's suit scanned the robot and made subtle changes in its own matte black structure.

"What do you want?" The Cyber warrior's voice was cold and emotionless, but spoke in perfect French, which Elle's suit proceeded to translate automatically.

"Like I said, a challenge."

The giantess stepped onto the platform's edge and stopped about ten yards away. "You're not from this city."

"What gave me away?" Eliana held her arms out to her sides, pretending to examine her outfit, but never taking her eyes off her opponent.

"You have no fear," the giantess replied without delay. "The rest of your kind hides in the dirt."

Eliana felt the rage climbing up her spine, trying to take control, but she resisted the bait. "Hides? Or is hunted?"

The robot shrugged. "For the weak it seems the same we suppose. We tried to tolerate humans. We even offer some leftover tech for those who prove themselves worthy. More than generous in our opinion." The warrior's face contorted into what looked like a snarl. "But you humans still don't seem to understand."

"What, how to become strong like Cyber?"

A halting laugh came in reply. "No, how to accept that you're weak. The world is ours now, [9]humans need to accept that, or die."

Eliana gestured down around her to the pile of wreckage on the dome beneath the platform. "Your drones didn't think I'm weak."

A plastic line which served as an eyebrow raised up. "Those things? Insects. They have no connection to the Singularity, just following orders."

"But you're different?"

This time it was the robot's turn to gesture down at her body. "Obviously."

"But soon you'll just be trash laying beside your cousins."

"We were wrong. You are no different than the rest of your kind, weak and disrespectful. It is time for you to learn your place."

"My place...is standing over the smoldering wreckage of your little metal puppet suit."

"Challenge accepted."

The robot reached down and pulled a massive silver blade out from the back of each leg, twirling them in front of her while her face remained passive. The display sped up until the blades were barely visible.

Eliana watched closely, waiting for her to stop showing off. When the blades finally halted in a classic sword fighting stance, Elle lifted her daggerlion up and extended its EMP rifle, which had been charging during their whole conversation.

One trigger pull and a massive pulse shot forth, expanding into a cone of electronic killing fury that swept through the giantess.

For a long second no one moved, then Eliana sprang forward, her cape billowing out behind her. At the peak of her jump, she planted both feet on the gleaming white chest and whirled her body into a massive sideways swipe with her blade. The slightly confused looking head toppled easily off its shoulders, and was caught in Elle's hands as it fell.

The Sky Princess stood on the massive torso, turning the head as it twitched into life. "You have no honor," it muttered, the voice coming out distant and strained.

"Maybe, but you're trash." Elle pointed the head down at its body and pinned it under one arm as she proceeded to eviscerate the carefully sculpted nano armor along with the wiring beneath. When she was done reducing the warrior to a sparking and smoking heap of destruction, she shoved it off the platform, making sure to let its head watch the entire process. Then she waved to the face as it rapidly lost power, and tossed it over her shoulder to join its friends.

Elle sat down, preparing to draw in more solar energy, when a glob of viscous green goop hit her shoulder. Pain sensors flared and then were dulled as the acid bit into her suit and the nanites in her bloodstream went to work neutralizing the poison.

She flung her cape up in a protective shield around her, spotting her assailants on her visual HUD display. A dozen mechanical raptors were corkscrewing down from the top of the nearby buildings, and more than a few were spitting globs of poison out from their beaks.

"You wanna fly? Let's fly."

Eliana burst out of hiding like a diver in reverse, folding into a tuck before twisting feet first into the air. The nearest raptor had a wing sliced neatly off its torso as she ascended. Once she leveled out, her cape formed back into jets and she blinked out of sight. In her wake, three venomous chunks collided, splattering droplets which ate their way through the platform when they landed.

The aerial Cyber challengers swooped up after her, only to find her plasma rifle rapidly firing down at them. Shards of steel exploded from wings as the fleet of raptors was quickly reduced to more falling wreckage.

Elle idly found herself thinking if more Banished would be left the task of cleaning up after the battle, and how many decades that may take.

Silence swept through the Arena area once again. Eliana remained hovering above the remains of the platform, head tilted back to let the sun hit her face. She spared a few seconds thinking about Leva up in the Anemoi, no doubt watching the battle intensely from up high. Elle made a little waving gesture at the clouds, then focused on recovery once again. The nanites had neutralized and disposed of the poison in her shoulder by now, and were working at stitching the hole in her suit back together.

Taking no chances at being surprised by another quick wave of reinforcements, she stretched her sensors' range to their utmost and waited, controlling her breathing to prepare for whatever came next.

It turns out she didn't need the sensors, because the next challenger announced herself long before getting close. A tiny figure with an amplified voice drifted closer.

"Sorry I'm late!" she called out cheerfully.

"My fault, I kind of just let myself in." Eliana squinted while trying to make out the details on the woman's face, then realized suddenly both who she was and why it was hard to see her. The naked pixie Champion was floating in a series of thick shimmering bubbles, and her miniscule body hid beneath multiple thick layers of bubble.

"How rude," she playfully chided. "I was headed over to another tournament in Berlin when Cyber called me back. Sounded rather urgent, too."

"So you're human?"

The pixie actually looked offended this time. "Yes, are you?"

"Touché." Elle ran full scans of the minuscule warrior, never letting her hand waver far from her weapon.

"Don't I look human?" She twirled in the bubble, showcasing her figure."

Elle laughed despite the tension between them. "You never can tell. The bot they sent out a few minutes ago looked every inch like a human...quite a bit taller than you though."

"Ahhh, they sent you a SAM?

"Sam?"

"Freakish swordswoman, samurai, ten feet tall?"

"She was a head shorter in the end, but yeah," Eliana nodded.

"Not a bad line of bots, but more or less obsolete nowadays. No-"

"Defense," Elle echoed her thought.

"Cyber's the best at mass production, but not very creative."

"And that's where you come in?"

"Hey, small is the new sexy." The pixie kicked back into a lazy back flip. Now are we ready to begin? I'm going to be late to Berlin as it is."

"Try me," Eliana snarled.

"No, no, I insist. Age before beauty."

"I've seen your last fight. You should leave now, or you will lose."

With that the Sky Princess thrust her daggerlion directly at the pixie, propelled forward by her suit. The blade was comically large compared to its target, the width nearly matching the pixie's entire height. But instead of piercing the translucent bubble, the weapon was deflected, throwing off Elle's balance.

As she recovered and brought her weapon up to block any counterattack, the pixie laughed, "Against that rhino meathead? I barely had to fight."

Eliana fired multiple EMP pulses at the bubbled enemy, doubting the trick would work twice.

"Tsk tsk, you didn't think it would be that easy, did you?"

The ranger simply shrugged, "seems we're at an impasse then. You're all defense and no offense."

The bubbles vibrated as the pixie got visibly angry. "Enough play, time to die, Feather." The outer membrane morphed and extended out rapidly towards Elle, and despite suffering three rapid slices, the bubble managed to fully envelope its prey.

Firing her ion jets at full power, Eliana's arms pushed against the thin membrane, but still it held.

"Too late for running away, little fly."

The air got siphoned out of the outer membrane in seconds, while the shimmering face of the pixie stared at Eliana. A wicked smile spread across her tiny face, waiting to watch the life drain out of yet another victim.

And Eliana just smiled right back at her. It didn't take the pixie long to realize her mistake, that the ranger's blood was brimming with oxygen producing nanites, but it was just long enough to seal her fate.

The Sky Princess had waited patiently, maneuvering her opponent, using her emotions against her, every step intentional. Now her suit exploded into a cloud of nanites, billowing out straight towards the increasingly alarmed pixie.

Where brute force had failed, the endlessly adaptive nanotech succeeded, analyzing each bubble layer and opening up holes to burrow through. They had shredded multiple layers before the pixie had the presence of mind to release her acid cloud attack. While her swarm of nano took some casualties, they mostly shrugged off the last ditch defense. And Eliana took a few seconds to heat the edge of her daggerlion to plasma levels, opening a neat gash behind her to slip out into fresh air once again.

Nanites penetrated the final bubbles surrounding the Champion, and the naked pixie writhed in pain as her acid cloud backfired on her. Iridescent skin began sloughing off the naked warrior, as faint screaming barely reached Elle as she hovered nearby. When the last bubble popped into mist, Eliana flew back down and absorbed as much of the nanotech as she could, then went to the arena platform to sit.

As she held a lotus position, her suit repaired itself, helped along by a handful of nanoinjections she retrieved from a bandolier across her chest. Soon a thundering chime rang out across the city, causing Eliana to open her eyes.

"A new warrior has proven herself worthy of being called Champion of Paris! Come and receive your reward."

Eliana exhaled slow and steady, glancing down at the dilating opening forming below her on the surface of the Dome. As it opened wider and wider, leaving room for an elaborate dias to rise up through it, Elle looked up at the clouds, waiting...

Chapter 6

Leva had been holding her breath the entire time Eliana was inside the pixie's outer bubble, less out of fear, although there was some of that, but more so due to anticipation. As the pixie finally dissolved, Leva locked in the autopilot for their Anemoi, eager to begin.

They knew that the Dome would likely open only when a new human Champion was crowned, and now it did so for Elle. It was unlike Cyber to make such an unforced error, but perhaps they were not as bound by their rules as humans thought. Or maybe some humans with power and influence were still tolerated by Cyber, and it was their vanity and greed which prompted the ceremony. After all, in the decades since the Singularity, there were never any significant rebellions, so there was little to fear from such minor indulgences.

When the circle had opened to its fullest diameter and the pedestal rose up, all hell broke loose.

The whole sky began to glow with reflected golden light. Huge thunderclouds formed from the shockwaves, then puffed away seconds later as a dozen wide beams of concentrated sunlight streaked down towards their shared target.

The Champion's award pedestal was instantly melted into slag. Heat from the combined beams funneled down into a vortex of destruction, and punched cleanly through the vulnerable opening in the Dome.

Leva watched as the scene unfolded far beneath her. Only when the entire city launched drone countermeasures did she drop out of her command position hovering nearly fifty thousand feet above the action.

As her Grand Anemoi descended, she ordered the platoon of Sky pilots to cut their beams and commence with suppressive fire.

The spines on her ship swept upwards, making it look like a metal comet as it accelerated towards the wreckage of the opening. Her backup did their best to clear the road for her, picking off hundreds of incoming drones using their spine EMP cannons. When she passed one hundred mph, she heard several impacts from drones exploding against her hull. Two hundred, three hundred mph, and the smoldering opening was coming up fast now. The ship was sustaining more damage from those unlucky enough or too slow to move out of her way.

Suddenly Leva shot into the gap, fires and live wires in all directions for just a second, and then she was through. Not wasting any time, she yanked back on an emergency brake lever, getting plastered against the bottom of her seat as internal organs lurched down towards her feet. Gravity outside of the oceans was unstable and prone to extremes, and Leva was still fighting nausea when she removed the harness, reached out and opened a hatch facing upwards.

Just before jumping out, she triggered the countdown on the ship's main weapon. As she fell away from the jagged spines, she saw them crackle with building electricity. As the Swarm zeroed in on her ship after its sudden appearance, Leva's mouth kept spreading wider and wider into a smile of righteous satisfaction. She was halfway between the Anemoi and the nearest rooftops when the spines could no longer contain the massive EMP pulse they were charging.

Normally an invisible weapon, the sheer force of this blast rippled the entire mass of air under the Dome as it expanded out at the speed of light. Thousands of bots, large and small, lost control in mid-air. The encroaching Swarm all took a nose dive at the same moment, and they let gravity take them down in great arcs converging beneath the ship.

Leva forced herself to look away from the sight so she could release her parachute and glide clear of the incoming wreckage. Even her

Anemoi fell, its circuitry damaged by the immense blast, and she heard as it impacted against a wide concrete avenue behind her.

Not only the Swarm was affected by the EMP. Both above and below, everything within a mile of the blast went back to the Stone Age. This included most of Old Paris, the newer skyscrapers, and a sizable chunk of the Dome. Darkness enveloped Leva as she tried to find her target landing zone. For a minute she began to panic as she couldn't spot any landmarks, but then a series of flares reoriented her.

She followed the line of flares, eventually landing in a small graveyard of an ancient church. At first only a handful of figures moved in the darkness, eerie red shadows from the flares trailing them as they emerged from a large mausoleum. By the time Leva touched down, Click had made her way over to meet her, back legs still raised to the sky with their EMP guns charged.

"Holy shit, Fish. You actually did it."

Leva couldn't help flashing a self satisfied grin, but her focus snapped back a second later. "Scuttle on back there and get the rest up here, now. There's not much time."

Click glared at the Princess as she quickly stowed her parachute back into her suit, but did as she was told. Back at the entrance to the mausoleum, Melter was already guiding dozens of Géos out into the graveyard. Within minutes, there were nearly four hundred scared people huddling together, with the thirty or so Arena fighters forming a perimeter with their eyes darting up above them.

Even the Elders had come, in their torn blue jeans and once white shirts, to risk everything for a chance at freedom. Whether that spoke of their trust for Eliana and Leva, or a complete desperation, it was hard to tell. But they came. They all came.

Leva called Click and a few of the lead fighters over to her. "Anything in that blast radius is scrap metal now, but we have to assume reinforcements are on their way."

A gaunt man in a leather jacket and numerous guns strapped to his limbs spoke up next. "Will they head to the ship first?"

"That's what I'm hoping," Leva answered. "So let's go away from there. Where's the nearest building that reaches up through the Dome?"

"Tour Cyber," Melter spat out. "Disgusting hunk of steel they put together early on. Quel dommage!"

Click nodded. "Five blocks east."

Leva stared in that direction and couldn't spot it, but the rest of them seemed to have no problem. Living underground seemed to have vastly improved their night vision. She made a mental note to ask Eliana to upgrade her vision before their next mission.

They headed out, filling the avenues in order to stay together and move as fast as possible. They made it halfway there before the first wave of drones found them.

Skimming past the rooftops nearby came first one, then dozens of dart shaped scouts. Their jets flared as they registered the heat signatures of so many humans, giving the Arena fighters just enough warning to prepare a counterattack.

Click's EMP guns silently targeted drone after drone, causing them to suddenly drop like stones. The leather jacket fighter opted for more traditional firepower. His muzzle blasts lit up the street in a near constant display of marksmanship. Nanoenhanced reflexes, Leva noted. Despite their best efforts though, multiple drones managed to release stunner bomblets, and many Géos were convulsing down on the pavement.

Groups of people managed to lift or assist the injured, and Leva pushed them all to keep moving. With a block left to go, the last scouts finally fell. There was nothing between them and the relative safety of the Tour Cyber except a courtyard still littered with burnt out husks from ancient gas fueled vehicles.

The first of the Géos had just entered the courtyard, when a sound like a chorus of jackhammers filled the darkness. Leva whipped her head back and forth, trying to spot the source, but Click simply sighed and motioned for the rest to back up.

The scorpion woman jumped into a tuck that continued as a fluid roll, taking her to the center of the clearing. She sprang out onto all four legs and raised her head to the sky. Her skin transformed into a chrome finish, with her lines of razor blades raised a couple of extra inches out from her armor.

Leva started to walk out after her, but the fighters held her back.

"Rollers," was muttered by a few. "She's got this."

Several large bots clanged their way into the courtyard a moment later. Each moved by rapidly rotating multiple rigid limbs. They climbed over rubble with ease, rolling forward like a pack of wolves. The leading Rollers rose up as they approached Click, preparing to bring their limbs down in devastating hammer blows.

When they came down, they all struck nothing but pavement, sparking in futility while trying to land a hit. Click slid under the front wave, slicing through supporting limbs on all sides, while her tail whipped upwards with surgical precision. Each movement found its mark, spilling oil and sending wires flying in all directions.

By the time the first three Rollers fell, she was already halfway through the next wave. The rest of the squadrons tried to regroup and surround the solo defender. While the Rollers pounded dents into the asphalt, none could shift side to side as quickly as Click. The scorpion tail spun nonstop, with a foot long blade at its end chopping through anything foolish enough to get within ten feet of her.

All that remained when Click stood back up was a few spasming legs which didn't realize they were detached from their owners. Leva stood in awe of the woman for a moment, then yelled out to the crowd behind her. "To the tower, now!"

Click's body softened back into its regular red leather body, with the lines of razors retracting almost to the skin. She was limping slightly, and looked depleted of energy, but the smile on her face told Leva she'd be fine.

Half of the Arena fighters entered the building first by pulling apart the deactivated sliding doors. The Elders were ushered inside next, followed by the children, then the rest of the Géoville population. Leva stayed back, helping any stragglers or injured make it to the doors safely. There was still no signal from Eliana, but they hadn't expected any while Leva was under the Dome.

As the last of the Géos entered Tour Cyber, a buzz began filling the air from far off.

"Reinforcements are here," is all Click said, her face grim. The sound grew louder and more insistent, like bees zeroing in on an intruder. They stepped inside the sliding doors, which despite their weight, seemed woefully unequal to the task of holding off the Swarm. With the elevator not working, and in the interests of keeping everyone together, they pushed their group into the emergency stairwell.

The front wave of the Swarm had reached the outer doors and were pushing tiny metal limbs in through the cracks. Others yanked on them, sacrificing the lead row, with their arms snapping off like twigs, in order to pry open the doors.

Chapter 7

Inside the pitch black stairwell, Leva was groping around frantically for anything to jam up against the door handle. A large hand gripped her shoulder, gently holding her in place for a moment.

Melter's huge frame nudged her aside and set to work. His fists began to glow a dull red, then brightened further until it was difficult to look at the blue flames dancing on them. He ran his fists along the seams of the door, severing limbs by the dozen, then as the doors snapped shut, he opened his hands and dug his fingers along the edges. His palms deformed the steel doors like wet clay, crimping them shut in several places within a minute.

"All better," he smirked, "let's go."

Leva didn't need any further prompting. She darted up the stairs after the trailing edge of the crowd. Fortunately, her suit gave off enough blue glow for her to see in the cramped quarters. It wasn't long before she heard screams from several floors up.

With no time to fight through the people clogging the stairs, she decided to skip them and leapt up onto the handrails. Leva crouched then jumped up, grabbing the floor of the next level. After pulling herself up and getting up onto the rails again, she repeated the process.

Twelve floors she ascended this way, driven onwards by the panic feeding off the sounds of more people falling to Cyber attackers. Her first glimpse of this new threat came from aluminum wings fluttering past her, followed by what looked like the body of a massive dragonfly. There were just too many doors to block them all off as they went, which allowed the highly maneuverable bots to enter the stairwell and wreak havoc.

A couple fighters managed to toss EMP grenades, but every dragonfly downed was replaced by another a few seconds later. By the time the first of the Géos reached the roof, a dozen more humans had fallen. Leva led the way, bursting through the doors into the blinding sunlight.

Explosions filled the sky in all directions, but her eyes still couldn't adjust to the brightness enough to see what was happening. The rest poured out the door after her, driven faster by their fear.

The concrete next to her strained with a loud thud, then a pair of strong hands grabbed her shoulders and shoved her roughly to the ground.

"Hit the deck, guppy!" Eliana shouted over the surrounding chaos.

Leva did as she was told. She knew better than to question her lover when she heard that tone of voice. She stayed huddled to the observation deck floor, trusting Elle to look out for them. While she ducked, her needle guns found easy targets.

As she was pulled back up to her feet by one hand on her collar, she felt lips roughly meet hers.

"You did amazing, but it's time to go." Elle gestured around the skyscraper, where multiple transport ships hovered, automatic rail guns firing nonstop. "Need a ride?"

From above them rays of light came pulsing with laser precision, strafing anything that came within ten city blocks of their building.

Click didn't need an invitation. She shuttled people from the rooftop door to the waiting transport ramps. Her back leg guns kept up some covering fire at first, but she quickly switched to using all four legs to help her people once she saw the firepower on display.

Melter hopped on board the nearest transport along with half the Elders, and a few fighters accompanied the other half on the next ship.

Wave after wave of Géos boarded the waiting ships, with the first ones to be full rocketing upwards to safety.

The last hundred people were huddled alongside the roof edge near the ships when the steel doors from the stairwell burst off their hinges. An explosion of white light from inside the doorway silhouetted a writhing mass of shadows.

Leva turned to the fleeing Géos and then back at Eliana who nodded grimly with the same thought. Without a word, the pair ran towards the light. As it faded, they got their first clear glimpse of the monstrosity.

Rapidly pulling itself up through the door frame and onto the roof was a seemingly endless metal snake. Thousands of hinged joints let it move with complete fluidity. There was no head to it, just hardened nanosteel that flattened to a razor edge at the front. Once fully emerged, it measured over fifty feet in length, and immediately slithered towards the crowd.

In unison, the Princesses attacked to draw its attention. Leva threw corrosive grenades which made it change course, but caused little actual damage. Elle was firing on the run with her EMP rifle, but the snake didn't even flinch. It might be nothing but nanosteel all the way to its core for all they knew, rendering EMP useless.

Guns were raised next, with Eliana switching over to exploding shells and Leva trying to slow it with nanosilk bombs. Both weapons proved much more effective. Multiple concentrated explosions blew holes along the leading edge, but it was closing the distance fast. Fortunately, the nanosilk pinned down the beast for a few precious seconds.

What happened next took both women off guard. Wherever the snake was held down or too damaged, it was managing to split itself, bifurcating so that a new razor flat head appeared and took a large section of snake along with it. Before long there were multiple smaller snakes, each one still several feet long, while small chunks were left behind.

A couple dozen refugees were left on the rooftop, so Elle and Leva continued their charge. Elle's daggerlion flashed like lightning, cutting through three of the nearest snakes with heavy clangs. While she watched the severed halves begin to reform yet again into yard long razors, Leva screamed out in pain.

One of the larger pieces of snake had coiled around the Mer's legs and was gouging deep cuts in a spiral as it grappled her.

Eliana was by her side a moment later, her fusion edged blade surgically slicing through the snake in a series of thrusting strikes. Then her world dripped with rage and she let out a savage snarl of challenge.

While guarding over Leva, the Sky general moved like a dancer from hell, fending off multiple whipping tails that were each capable of ending both their lives. At every opportunity, Elle issued counterattacks, mincing the nanosteel into smaller and smaller pieces.

And still they came. Despite having not many snakes longer than a foot long, they all attacked with one mind, staggering their timing to maximize their chances.

But Elle was done with this exhausting battle, and needed to get Leva safely off the roof. The Mer was able to stand, but her legs were bleeding profusely, and she didn't have long before she'd pass out.

Making a command decision as only a battle hardened soldier could, Eliana grabbed Leva by the ribs and lifted her up.

"Trust me," was all she said before launching Leva upwards as far as she could. Then right as the Mer reached the top of her arc ten feet above the fray, Elle triggered her powerful electric pulse from her suit. It was the same one that had thrown Click into a wall when they first met, and against such lighter opponents, it had quite a bit more dramatic effect.

The encroaching mass of snakes were blasted across the rooftop concrete in all directions. The closest ones didn't even make it that far. As electricity built up in their tiny conductive bodies, they exploded with sizzling pops.

A few seconds after tossing Leva, it was all over, and Elle caught her lover. No transports were left, meaning the last of the refugees had escaped. Eliana's cape flared out into a cone beneath them and they were airborne. The Anemoi were still strafing the area, but had been forced to give the rising transports a wide berth.

Eliana flew them up away from the fiery scene below, and finally felt herself relax enough to savor the rush of wind past her face. Leva was grimacing, and took the opportunity to grab a black plastic tube from her waistband. A sequence of buttons triggered a syringe to extend, which she immediately thrust into her thigh. The nanobooster would help her wounds halt the bleeding and begin the process of reknitting flesh.

After reaching a height of nearly thirty thousand feet, they found the Sky fleet waiting. A couple of transports showed signs of damage, but nothing major, and a brand new Grand Anemoi awaited the Princesses.

Click leaned out of the nearest ship as they rose past, giving them both a salute and a smirk of grudging respect. They were on their way back to the Sky Council to deliver a report in person of Cyber's intentions and capabilities, as well as to receive their next assignment.

As for Click and the Géos, they were temporarily being taken to one of the largest underwater cities of the Mer, since the daylight was still too much for their eyes to tolerate. Located out in the Atlantic, it was thought to be a safe place for them to recuperate while they all decided where amongst the Sky and Mer they wished to live. Most of the arena fighters were ready to help in the fight against Cyber, but wanted to make sure their people were settled first.

Elle made sure that she and Leva were thoroughly off the grid for a solid week this time. Her neural link was turned off, letting the women bask in the quiet peacefulness of an abandoned Sky outpost, cruising along with the northern jetstream.

Leva's legs were fully healed within the first two days of course, especially with the help of top grade nano, but Eliana wanted to give her a vigorous, and secluded, physical therapy routine. She had personally experienced the strength those thighs were capable of producing, and made sure she was moving at full capacity before they started any more insane diplomatic missions.

When Elle finally relented to Leva's persistent questions about whether there was any word on where the Géos chose to settle, she was bombarded with a dozen glaring notifications in her retinal HUD. This sort of overriding intrusive messaging could only mean one thing: the Sky Council needed them. Immediately.

With a smug grin, Leva took her official blue chiffon Sky robe from a deflated looking Elle who had already changed into her own.

"Just, shut it. We gotta go." Elle grimaced, drawing a laugh from her partner.

They arrived in the upper atmosphere at the Heaven's Watch stronghold nearly two hours later, and were allowed to land much closer to the citadel this time. However, instead of being brought before the entire Sky Council, they appeared to be guided towards a much smaller structure, a private residence of one of the Seven Sky Queens. Their crystalline guides were a small flock of translucent birds, security drones with advanced tech.

They reached the threshold of a large oval shaped building, unassuming in stature except for the quality of the material making up its walls. The house seemed to adapt its coloring to every change in sunlight, and it flexed its entire design in response to each passing gust of wind.

Eliana entered first after removing her boots, then turned and coaxed the nervous Leva into following. Elle bowed immediately upon spotting Queen Windritch, and held there awaiting her Elder's words. Leva copied the movement. It was the only time Leva could recall seeing Elle show such respect.

"Rise, girls." The gravelly yet feminine voice put them both at ease. The Queen wore a simple leather tunic, with her wings dovetailed expertly into each other, forming a velvety black halo behind her. Her feet were not actual claws as Leva had assumed they were, but instead were smallish amber feet which looked weathered as if they had rarely ever stayed indoors.

Leva nervously glanced around the room, not knowing what to do with herself or if she should even be included in whatever conversation was about to happen.

"What's the matter? Did you expect a nest?"

Leva blushed crimson, "no, ma'am, I mean Queen. I didn't know what to expect, to be honest."

"Enough of this. Come, sit down. We have much to discuss. But first, let me welcome the last of our party."

In behind them through the threshold came two pairs of staccato footsteps, which didn't require taking off any shoes since they never wore any.

"Well if it isn't my two puffy Princesses again."

Eliana's whole body visibly tensed, not only for having a newcomer in the presence of the esteemed Councilwoman, but also for having to wear her gauzy blue diplomatic dress in front of the gruff scorpion woman.

Windritch observed their interaction carefully before continuing her walk over to a massive holo projection table.

"Now, Click. Your people have all been relocated to Cymopoleia."

"Those that survived the escape, yes. Forty were not so lucky."

Windritch darted her eyes straight at Click, gauging her intentions.

"Yes, I understand forty seven of your people died seeking their freedom. We all mourn their deaths, but as you well know, with Cyber on the offensive, no one in Géoville would have survived for much longer."

Click begrudgingly nodded. "I don't regret our escape, but I honor them by reminding you of their passing."

The Queen huffed. "Child, I do not have time for such petty games. Do not lecture me on the sanctity of human life. I've been in charge of defending humanity against those metal sons of bitches since before you were born."

Click smiled broad and relaxed before turning to the Princesses. "I like her."

"Yes, an honor, I'm sure."

"Elder, why have you summoned us here?" Eliana took back control of the room decorum. "Surely you must have news to share."

"Indeed." She pulled up a holo display of Paris, with everything from its Arena in the sky to the subterranean community. "Now we had already heard of Géoville due to its location in such a famous city."

Now she flicked her hand towards the display and widened it out until the whole Earth was seen swirling inside the house.

"What we hadn't heard of before now, is the number of other such human sanctuaries."

Another wrist flick, and hundreds of dots blinked into existence across the globe. From every corner of every continent, people were still alive. Click and the Princesses were reeling from the knowledge, unable to speak for a moment. Finally Leva got her lips to move enough to ask, "How? So many, why haven't we known?"

Queen Eldritch pursed her wrinkled lips. "Once again it seems our newfound intel is a result of your actions. And dumb luck," she ended flatly. After changing back to a holo of Paris, she played a reenactment of Leva's Anemoi plunging into the gap of the Dome. A visible bubble of light expanded out from it, representing the massive EMP pulse.

"Your reckless stunt got the attention of more than just Cyber. It also damaged a new group of humans operating on the outskirts of Paris."

"There were others, in the city?" Click asked, stunned.

"Not in the city itself, but outside the Dome. They call themselves the Leeches. They've managed to survive by tapping into the overground cable lines crisscrossing the planet. Much like the underwater cables we discovered, except these are much thinner, much less protected and damn near everywhere."

"The cables helped them survive?" Eliana prodded.

"Yes, they siphon energy from them, spreading it out so Cyber dismisses it as standard signal strength loss. But that's not all." Queen Windritch let the possibilities linger unanswered while she took a deep, measured breath. "They hacked into the Cyber Singularity."

All three younger women reacted in disbelief.

"No one has ever been able to decipher their code," Click said, trying to sound as conclusive as possible, but with doubt creeping in.

"Their encryption is far beyond human capabilities," Elle said, "I thought."

"We have all adapted in different ways to this new world we live in." The Queen spread her wings out a bit to ruffle them. "The Leeches are no exception. Apparently they have modified their own brains more than we thought possible. Click, I believe you have such an enhancement."

Click nearly snorted, "Ha, yeah, I have synaptic enhancements, helps my reflexes and memory storage. But nothing like Cyber, their tech...it's like magic."

"Degrees, all a matter of degrees, my dears. And once one community was able to break their encryption, they sent out signal codes, which in turn were picked up by other such survivors around the world. They used Cyber's own network against them, and now we know of more than four hundred groups associated with the Leeches."

"So I still don't understand, why haven't we known about them until now?" Leva asked, confused.

"They live their lives mostly in a digital world, and until now, they had no idea that we existed either."

Eliana could sense the question hanging over them. She could feel it ever since the moment they walked inside.

"So what now? Are we supposed to go visit four hundred different Leech hideouts? Airlift them out?"

"By the gods, please no. Everywhere you go turns into a smoldering pile of wreckage."

Click snorted at that comment, which caused Eliana to defend herself, but then Leva stopped her with a shrug.

"She's not wrong."

Still bristling with indignation, but secretly a little proud of such a reputation, Elle spat out, "Then what? What's the plan?"

The Queen sat against a crystal railing, smiling. "They have a plan, actually. But they need our help. They think they have a way to cripple Cyber, break the Singularity. But in order to do so, they need to get access to one of the most secure locations on the planet."

"They have a virus?" Click guessed.

"Yes. But they need a couple of insane Princesses and a Scorpion to get them where they need to go."

No one spoke for a prolonged pause. The women all exchanged glances before looking back at the Queen.

"Sign us up!"

About The Author

David Colello[1] is an ecopunk prophet, making badass lemonade out of apocalyptic lemons, and squinting hard to see the good. Following his time at Boston University earning degrees in English and Philosophy, he owned a personal training studio, worked in freelance copywriting, became a stay home father to three little future punks, and now publishes science fiction for a world where wonder is in short supply.

---

1. http://www.davidcolello.com

If you enjoyed Skypunk Princess, please consider giving it a rating and review.

For sneak peeks and a chance to receive the next books *FREE* before they get released, sign up to the **Secret Early Readers List** on my website, www.davidcolello.com[2].

---

2. http://www.davidcolello.com